Meet Lydia

For my grandparents,
for the kids of the present,
and those yet to come. —MBL

Council Oak Books, 2105 E. 15th St., Suite B, Tulsa, OK 74104

Project Director and Head of Publications, NMAI: Terence Winch
Series Editor, NMAI: Sally Barrows
Series Design Concept: Andrea L. Boven, Boven Design Studio, Inc.
Cover and Interior Design: Barbara Leese and Jerry Soga

The Smithsonian National Museum of the American Indian is dedicated to working in collaboration with the indigenous peoples of the Americas to preserve, study, and exhibit the life, languages, literature, history, and arts of the Native peoples of the Western Hemisphere. The museum's publishing program seeks to augment awareness of Native American beliefs and lifeways, and to educate the public about the history and significance of Native cultures.

The museum on the National Mall in Washington, D.C., is one of the leading cultural destinations in the world. The museum's George Gustav Heye Center is one of New York City's premier museums. The Cultural Resources Center in Suitland, Maryland, houses the museum's collection and serves as a research and conservation facility.

For information about the National Museum of the American Indian, visit www.AmericanIndian.si.edu. For information about becoming a member of NMAI, call 800-242-6624.

On the half-title page: Dancer's bib, beaded with the image of an eagle, part of the Wooshkeetaan, or Shark, clan regalia.

First edition
10 9 8 7 6 5 4 3 2 1

LIBRARY OF CONGRESS CATALOGING-IN-PUBLICATION DATA
Belarde-Lewis, Miranda.
    Meet Lydia : a native girl from southeast Alaska / by Miranda
Belarde-Lewis ; with photographs by John Harrington.— 1st ed.
        p. cm. — (My world—Young Native Americans today)
    ISBN 1-57178-147-1
  1. Mills, Lydia—Juvenile literature. 2. Tlingit Indians—Social life and customs—Juvenile literature.
3. Tlingit Indians—Biography—Juvenile literature. [1. Mills, Lydia. 2. Tlingit Indians—Biography.
3. Indians of North America—Alaska—Biography.] I. Harrington, John, 1966- ill. II. Title. III. Series.

  E99.T6B45 2004
  979.8004'9727'0092—dc22
                                        2003027396

A Note about the Tlingit Language
The Tlingit language has one of the most complex sound systems in the world.
It includes twenty-four sounds not shared with English, and four of its sounds are
not found in any other language on earth. The English alphabet had to be modified
for writing Tlingit, so the pronunciations given in this book provide only a rough
idea of what a speaker with a heavy English accent would say.
                —*Miranda Belarde-Lewis*

Meet Lydia

A Native Girl from Southeast Alaska

Miranda Belarde-Lewis

with photographs by
John Harrington

My World: Young Native Americans Today

Smithsonian National Museum of the American Indian
in association with
Council Oak Books

K esh'shi, Ho' le'shina (pronounced KEHSH-she, HOTE-let-shee-nah) Miranda Belarde-Lewis. Miranda Belarde-Lewis, *yóo x̱at duwasáakw* (pronounced YOO-hut-dew-wuh-sock).

Both of these phrases mean, "Hello, my name is Miranda Belarde-Lewis."

My parents have different backgrounds, but they are both Native American. My mom is Tlingit (pronounced KLING-ket) and Filipino, and my dad is Zuni (pronounced ZOO-nee) and Cherokee (pronounced CHAIR-oh-kee). They met while in college in Colorado. Although my brother, Raven, and I grew up in Zuni, New Mexico, our family spent several weeks every summer visiting our relatives in Alaska. Raven and I are lucky to have strong and loving family ties to two very different cultures.

There are more than five hundred Native American communities just in the United States. Many people think that they are all the same. This is not true, although many have similar traditions and ideas.

Zuni Pueblo, a village within the Zuni reservation, is right next to the Arizona/New Mexico border. We call ourselves the A:shiwi (pronounced AH-she-we) or Shiwi. About ten thousand Shiwi people live in Zuni. When Spanish explorers came through what is now known as New Mexico in the early 1500s, they probably misheard our name, and called us Zuni. Now everyone knows us by that name. Our reservation is 259 square miles, which is a little bigger than the city of Chicago. We have lived on our land for thousands of years.

Although our homelands are at a high elevation, the landscape is very flat. Our mountains have flat tops, so the Spanish called them mesas, or tables. The trees around Zuni are chubby and grow close to the ground. We get some snow in the winter, but during the summer it can sometimes be as hot as 100 degrees.

LEFT: For thousands of years, Zuni people have been successfully growing corn, squash, and beans in the desert soil. This photo shows a garden that is planted in a waffle-like grid pattern, an ancient irrigation method that helps to keep water around the base of each plant. (NMAI P18811)

RIGHT: Pueblo is the Spanish word for "village," but it also means groups of houses built on top of one another, like apartment buildings. (NMAI P18817)

Alaska looks very different from New Mexico. The southeast part of Alaska is a group of peninsulas and islands right next to Canada. The landscape alternates between large bodies of water and huge, tree-covered mountains. Rain comes easily—sometimes for weeks! Often the fog on the water is so thick that it blocks the view of the mountains directly in front of you. The trees grow very tall, with branches strong enough to hold a bald eagle's nest, which can be as big and heavy as a jeep! Bears, moose, bald eagles, otters, ravens, and seals appear almost everywhere, even in the city of Juneau (pronounced JOO-know), Alaska's state capital.

My mom's family and their Tlingit community live in Juneau or in island villages across the water. A lot of our extended family still live in a village called Hoonah, where many of them were born. When we visited in the summer, my family would stay with my Grandma Sue in Juneau. We also spent time with other relatives—in Hoonah and at another place called Excursion Inlet.

A bald eagle perched in a fir tree. Because this one is young, its head hasn't yet turned white.

ABOVE: A ferry that takes people and cars around the waterways of southeast Alaska. It takes about three hours to travel by ferry from Juneau to the village of Hoonah. (Photo by David Sheakley [Tlingit])

Travel to most towns and villages in southeast Alaska is not possible in a car, even though each town has its own paved roads. If you want to take your car, you have to put it on a ferryboat. Otherwise, planes, ferries, and smaller boats are the only way to get from island to island. My cousins, my brother, and I had fun on the boats, but planes are much faster.

I want to introduce you to one of my cousins. Her name is Lydia. She lives in Juneau, but she has been traveling to Hoonah and Excursion Inlet since she was a baby. She will tell you about her life in southeast Alaska and about some of the things we do as Tlingit people.

*L*ydia Mills *yóo xat duwasáakw* (pronounced YOO-hut-dew-wuh-sock). This phrase means, "Hi, my name is Lydia Mills." My Tlingit name is Tléikw shagoon (pronounced KLAKE-shuh-GOON). It means "putting up berries" or "the ancestor of a berry."

I'm ten years old and in the fifth grade. I have an older brother named Thomas. We spend the school year in Juneau with my mom. In the summer and on school breaks, we stay with my dad in Hoonah, at Excursion Inlet, or at our cabin near another town called Gustavus (pronounced gus-DAVE-us).

My mom is not Tlingit. Her parents are German and French-English. She grew up in Los Angeles, but when she was in graduate school she worked at Excursion Inlet for a summer. She met my dad there, while he was fishing for the family. After she finished school, she married him and moved up here to Alaska.

My parents divorced when I was three. Other kids at my school also have parents who are divorced. It makes me sad that my parents aren't together anymore, but at least my mom and dad can still be friends.

My dad lives in Hoonah and works for a company that loads logs onto ships. He still fishes for himself and the family, and he teaches my brother and me about nature and respect for nature. I like spending the summer with my dad, but during the school year, I have lots to do in Juneau.

LEFT: Lydia in front of her dad's cabin near Gustavus.

RIGHT: Lydia's father, Thomas Mills Sr., at work on a logging ship in the harbor at Hoonah. (Courtesy of the Mills family)

I t's difficult to say how many Tlingit people lived in southeast Alaska before
Europeans arrived in the 1700s, because we were dispersed throughout hundreds
of islands. Today about fifteen thousand of us are spread out in towns and villages
all over the region. Some of us live in areas as far away as Seattle, which is about
900 miles to the south.

When different groups of Europeans started exploring the area, they tried various
ways of controlling the Native peoples they encountered. The Russians learned
Native languages so they could try to convert people to Christianity. American missionaries came later—after the United States government bought Alaska from Russia
in 1867. They wanted to bring their version of civilization and organized religion to
Native people. Neither the Russian nor the American missionaries respected the
Tlingits' complicated social rules and religious practices, which had evolved long
before the first Europeans got to Alaska.

ABOVE RIGHT: An outline map of Alaska, highlighting the southeastern part of the state.

ABOVE MIDDLE: A map of southeast Alaska. (Courtesy of NG Maps/National Geographic Image Collection)

ABOVE LEFT: A map of the towns and villages where Lydia spends time: Juneau, Hoonah, Gustavus, and Excursion Inlet. (Courtesy of NG Maps/National Geographic Image Collection)

OPPOSITE: Russian clergy and congregation stand in front of St. Michael's Russian Orthodox Cathedral in Sitka, Alaska, c. 1917. The Tlingit men are wearing sashes for two different church brotherhoods. (Courtesy of the Alaska State Library Historical Collections, PCA 57-48)

*D*uring the school year I'm very busy, but before I do all of my other activities, I have to finish my schoolwork. We study math, writing, spelling, and reading. I don't like math, but I still do it. My favorite subject is the history of early humans. I especially like learning about Neanderthals because they were smart, big, and strong.

I play soccer on the No Fear team. We practice during the week and play against other Juneau teams on the weekends. The weather is so rainy most of the time that we have all of our games indoors. Sometimes we win by a lot but other times we don't score any goals. I want to keep playing soccer when I go to middle school next year.

I've been playing the trombone in our school music class for two-and-a-half years. I like the trombone because it's a unique instrument that not many of my friends can play.

I became a Girl Scout at about the same time I started playing the trombone. I like selling cookies, going on sleepovers with the other Scouts, and earning badges. Earning the Camp Feather badge was fun because Girl Scouts from Ketchikan and Sitka, two other towns in southeast Alaska, came by ferry to Juneau and stayed for four days. We tie-dyed tee shirts and made our own friendship books.

OPPOSITE TOP: Lydia and her classmate Denali Hyatt learn the square root system in their Montessori classroom.

OPPOSITE MIDDLE: Lydia and her brother Thomas practice soccer after school on the beach near their house in Juneau.

OPPOSITE BOTTOM: Lydia plays the trombone during a rehearsal of the fifth-grade play.

*E*very Wednesday morning, I help in the language enhancement kindergarten class at my school. The teachers, Kitty Eddy and Nancy Douglas, speak Tlingit in class and try to encourage the kids to speak Tlingit, too. Everything in the classroom has an English name and a Tlingit name. Paper snowflakes and raindrops are hung around the room, and they, too, are labeled in English and Tlingit.

Almost every week an elder called Grandpa Milton and his wife, Betty, visit the kindergarten class when I'm there. They teach us songs in Tlingit and tell us stories. I also read books about nature to the kindergarteners. When the books describe fish, I show them what kinds of fish my brother Thomas and I catch during the summer.

When Kitty and Nancy asked if I would help in their class, something in me just said to go there. I'm the only Tlingit person in my fifth-grade class, and sometimes I feel lonely and start to miss my dad. Being around the kids, our language, and Kitty and Nancy makes me feel better. When I'm helping the younger kids with their projects, they teach me words I don't yet know, so we learn Tlingit together.

Lydia reads to the Tlingit language enhancement class.

When American missionaries first came to southeast Alaska, they set up schools for Native kids where speaking any language but English was strictly forbidden. As a girl, Lydia's grandmother, Katherine Mills, attended a school where the teachers would wash out her mouth with soap if they caught her speaking Tlingit. These schools existed for such a long time that several generations of Tlingit people grew up barely able to speak or understand our own language. By the 1970s, schools weren't run by missionaries anymore, and some of the elders who remembered Tlingit (from speaking it at home) began to teach what they knew. Katherine Mills was one of the first people to introduce the Tlingit language into Alaska's schools and universities. During the 1970s and 1980s, she taught Tlingit language and culture classes all over Alaska, including at the high school in Hoonah. Together with some of her students, she published a math book to help them remember the words for animals, plants, and numbers.

BELOW: A page from Grandma Katherine's Tlingit math book that shows how to spell the numbers for counting animals and objects. The numbers for counting humans are spelled differently. (Courtesy of the Mills family)

Jinkaat ch'áak' aas yíkt ḵéen.

Nás'k át kawdliyeech.

X'oon ch'áak' sá áwoo tle wóoshteen?

__10__ + __3__ = __13__

jinkaat ḵa nás'k

ABOVE: Native Alaskan students at the Sheldon Jackson School in Sitka pose for their class picture, which was taken in the early 1900s. (Courtesy of the Alaska State Library Historical Collections, PCA 57-5)

ince kindergarten, I've been dancing with the culture club at my school. It's called Juneau Indian Studies, and it includes kids from southeast Alaska's other two Native groups, Haida (pronounced HIDE-ah) and Tsimshian (pronounced SIM-shee-an). We get together once a week after school to hear traditional stories, work on art projects that display our clan crests, and learn songs. When we have performances coming up, we meet more often to practice our dances.

Boys and girls are taught different ways of dancing. My brother and the other boys hop around like ravens on the beach. The other girls and I put our hands on our hips as we dance. My dad once told me that the people in my clan—the Wooshkeetaan (pronounced woosh-key-tahn), or Shark Clan—dance with our hands in front of us, palms up, as a sign of peace. This is because the Wooshkeetaans were known as a warrior clan, but while we were dancing we wanted to show that we wouldn't attack.

The culture club in front of the totem pole at Dzantik'i Heeni (pronounced TSAN-tee-key-HEE-nee) Middle School.

LEFT: Thomas, Lydia, and their aunt, Judy Brown, rehearsing the Tlingit National Anthem with the middle school culture club. Lydia has already performed with this group, and next year, when she starts middle school, it will be her regular culture club.

RIGHT: Lydia's uncle, Greg Brown, the culture club's instructor, wearing his Teikweidi (pronounced take-way-DEE), or Bear Clan, regalia.

Tlingit people separate themselves into two groups—the Eagles and the Ravens. Each side is made up of many clans. Tlingits use a matrilineal system, which means that we inherit our mother's clan. Traditionally, Tlingits have to marry someone from the opposite side to keep the community balanced. Since Wooshkeetaans are part of the Eagle half of the community, it would be best if Lydia married a Raven when she grows up.

When we dance, we wear our regalia, our ceremonial clothing. Our regalia shows others who we are and how proud we are to be Tlingit, Haida, or Tsimshian. Our moms, aunts, and grandmas make our regalia for us. We get to keep these pieces and, if we take care of them, we will pass them on to our children. Regalia can be masks, headbands, vests, hats, bags, robes, or blankets with buttons attached.

Tlingit clans also can own special ceremonial regalia. This kind of regalia is shared by everyone in the clan and is part of the clan's *at.tóow* (pronounced uht-OOW), or property. In addition to regalia, at.tóow includes songs, stories, dances, and artistic designs. We bring out our at.tóow at special events so that we can all see it. The clothing and carved pieces are usually really old and can refer to stories about how our clan came to be. When at.tóow is not being displayed, one of the clan's most responsible people takes care of it. After Grandma Katherine died, the elders of my dad's clan asked him to take the job of keeping the T'akdeintaan (pronounced duck-dane-taan), or Seagull, clan property.

OPPOSITE TOP: Traditionally, the yarn for chilkat robes like this one was made of mountain goat hair and shredded cedar bark. Other Tlingit weavings evolved from basket weaving, but chilkat designs are copied from paintings on boards and are more difficult to weave because they include curved lines.

OPPOSITE MIDDLE: Lydia holds a blanket beaded with a shark emblem, her clan symbol. This blanket is part of the Wooshkeetaan clan regalia and is displayed or worn only on special occasions.

OPPOSITE BOTTOM: This headpiece, topped with long white ermine tails, tells a story about a part of the Seagull Clan called Snail House. Only Snail House members have the right to tell this story. If anyone else told it, he or she would have to pay a fine.

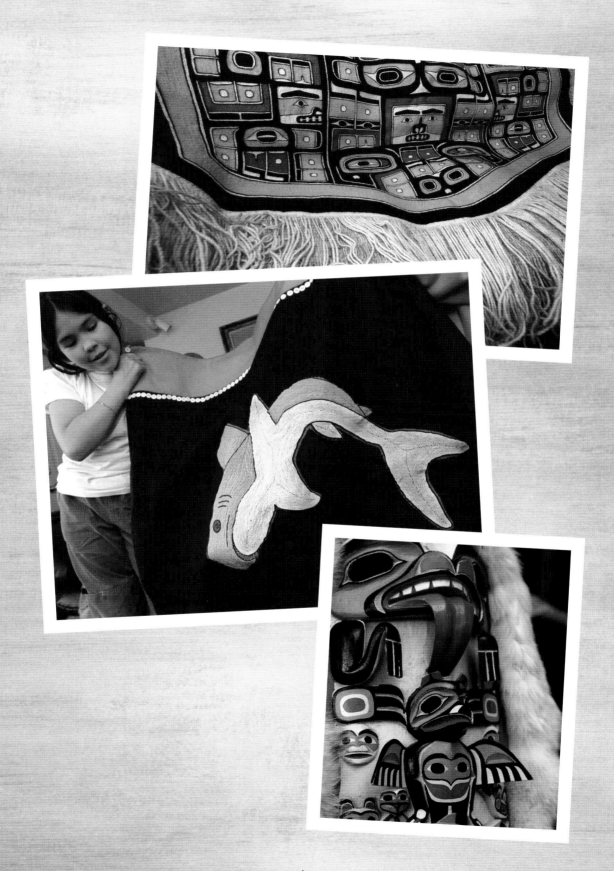

*C*lan property takes many shapes and forms. Bentwood boxes are made from thin sheets of wood that are bent to form the box's corners. Drums and paddles can be held while you're dancing.

Another kind of at.tóow is songs. Every clan has its own songs, stories, and dances. When Grandma Katherine was born, her dad wrote a song for her. Today people from other villages know my grandma's song, and they sing it to honor her. I don't really remember Grandma Katherine, but I've heard so much about her that I miss her.

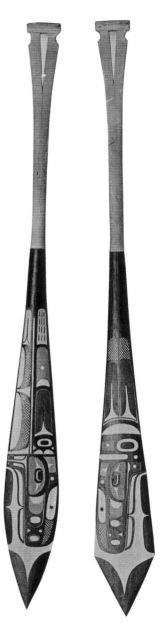

RIGHT: Traditionally, larger boat paddles could be carved so that they had a sharp point. That way, they could be used not only to paddle a boat but also as a weapon. Small paddles can be used in dances to help tell the story of the song and add emphasis to movements, because Tlingit dances aren't as flashy as some other Native dances. (NMAI L00567)

ABOVE: A bentwood box made of cedar. The sides of the box and the lid are each made from just one piece of wood, so the box has no seams at the corners. This one is from the town of Sitka. (NMAI N33702)

LEFT: An eagle figure carved into the bottom of a house post. House posts were built into the walls at either end of a clan house. They are wider at the top than totem poles, so they can support a roof.

FAR RIGHT: This totem pole, which stands in front of the elementary school in Hoonah, is carved with sea creatures. At the bottom is the figure of a fisherman. (Carved by Rick Beasley, Mick Beasley, and Steve Brown.)

RIGHT: The fisherman at the bottom of the totem pole is carrying a special tool called a halibut hook, which is used to catch the big, heavy fish.

Carving clan symbols into pieces of wood is a very old tradition with Tlingit people. Because we live in a rainforest, Tlingits and other Native people in the area are expert woodworkers. We are especially famous for carving totem poles. Totem poles are generally made to show our clan or cultural identity. A totem pole can honor a person who has died; help people remember a story; or stand as a welcoming pole in front of a house, school, or community center. Because Tlingits relied on animals to survive, animals are the most common forms carved on totem poles. Some people think that totem poles are religious objects for Tlingits, but we have never worshipped the poles or the symbols on them.

Celebration is a three-day festival to honor southeast Alaska's Native peoples. It was started in 1982 and takes place every two years. It helps us continue our customs because the Tlingit, Haida, and Tsimshian share a lot of the same ideas about how to express our cultures. The festival, which takes place in and around Juneau's convention center, begins and ends with big parades. Each day you can watch different dance groups perform, buy foods such as salmon and seaweed, and shop for small things, such as dolls and bags. Dance groups from all over the region are invited, and every Celebration is bigger than the last.

LEFT: The big Celebration parade winds through downtown Juneau. (Photo by David Sheakley [Tlingit])

OPPOSITE: Dance groups from all over Alaska, the continental United States, and Hawai'i prepare to rush the stage at Centennial Hall for the opening ceremonies of Celebration. During the ceremonies, dancers pack the hall, and most groups stand on the floor surrounding the stage. The first groups that enter lead the opening song, which means that they sing and dance without stopping for more than an hour, until all the other groups have arrived. (Photo by David Sheakley [Tlingit])

When I was really little, I used to sit on my dad's shoulders and watch the dances, but during the past two Celebrations, my brother and I took part in the dances with our culture club. About six weeks before each Celebration, the club began meeting three times a week to practice. At the last Celebration we performed our dances about twice a day on each of the three days. Our practicing paid off, because everyone told us we did a really good job. Dancing so much made me feel exhausted but proud.

Celebration is a chance for all of us to show pride in being Alaska Natives. It's also a chance to display individual, group, and village talent. It's a time to hear stories, eat good food, and meet friends. It's also a time to show off our new and old regalia. I love wearing my blankets and singing in my own language.

OPPOSITE TOP: The Hoonah dance group at the end of the parade at Celebration. For last year's Celebration, some of Lydia's cousins from Hoonah came to Juneau with their dance group. The group is called Gaax̱w X'aayi (pronounced GAWK hi-YEE), which means "Duck Point."

OPPOSITE BOTTOM: Lydia and Thomas after a Celebration parade. Lydia is wearing two regalia bags that her mother made.

*I*n the past, a big party known as a potlatch was a way for someone to show how generous he or she was. If a family had luck catching fish, hunting deer and seal, and picking berries, they would share their food at a potlatch. Everyone in their village would be invited. People would put on their regalia, tell stories, sing and dance, and eat together. The more the hosts gave away, the more respect and honor they brought to themselves, their family, and their village.

Potlatches are different from each other because each clan has different traditions. They often are memorial parties held one or even several years after a family member has died and a funeral has taken place. The Tlingit word for this kind of potlatch is _koo.éex'_ (pronounced khoo-EEK). Memorial parties start with mourning songs and speeches. People from different clans offer words of encouragement to the clan that has lost a family member.

After the speeches, the serious mood begins to change. Food is served, and gifts are offered. There is always food at a _koo.éex'_, both to take home and to eat. Sometimes you can eat four meals at one memorial party! Traditional Tlingit food includes cooked and smoked salmon, boiled herring eggs (they're tiny and crunch like bubble wrap when you eat them), seal meat, deer meat stew, and seaweed stew made with salmon eggs. For dessert we have berry stew: a big tub filled with all different kinds of freshly picked berries. Most potlatches are filled with song and dance, and they last almost all night. A few even last for twenty-four hours.

OPPOSITE LEFT: Thomas (center), helping his cousins, Michael Mills Jr. (left) and William Mills (right) at a memorial potlatch for their Grandpa Gilbert held many years ago. They are bringing in a big tub of berries. After this picture was taken, Thomas was lifted into the air while still hanging onto the tub. All of the guests were laughing so hard that they almost fell off their seats. (Courtesy of the Mills family)

OPPOSITE RIGHT: At most potlatches, the giveaways are so generous that everyone needs a box to carry away all of their gifts. This is a memorial party for Lydia's Uncle Gilbert "Butch" Mills Jr., which Lydia attended when she was just a baby. (Courtesy of the Mills family)

Memorial potlatches also mark other changes, such as adoption. When a Tlingit person marries someone who is not Tlingit, the new person can be adopted by the Tlingit family. After the giveaway, the Tlingit person announces his or her reasons for inviting the newcomer into the clan. They give the adoptee a Tlingit name, and the crowd repeats the name three times, both to remember it and to make the adoption official. After that, the new person is seen as a member of the Tlingit people.

After Lydia's mom married her dad, her Grandpa Gilbert, who was of the Shark Clan, adopted her during a potlatch. Lydia's mom helped serve food all night, and then her father-in-law gave her money to give away to the guests, to thank them for being witnesses to her adoption. Because clans are matrilineal, Thomas and Lydia are of the Shark Clan, too.

I'm lucky that my mom helps Thomas and me to learn about our Tlingit culture. She even takes classes at the University of Alaska to learn more. She also makes regalia for us. She can weave ravenstail, a really old geometric pattern, and she even made me an octopus bag that I wore at last year's Celebration.

Once a week I go to a beading class at a shop in downtown Juneau. When I first started, I had to take one beading class from Salty, the owner. After that, I could go to the free beading circle for kids on any Thursday. I've been going for three years. I like to make bracelets and necklaces on the loom.

ABOVE: Lydia chooses beads and works on a bracelet at her beading class, while Salty Hanes, the bead shop owner, watches.

ABOVE: Lydia wears an octopus bag and a ravenstail bag made by her mother. Since the octopus bag has eight glovelike fingers, it's easy to understand the origins of its name.

ABOVE: Lydia and her mother work together on a partially finished bag for Thomas. Lydia's mom says that Lydia naturally twists her yarn in the same way as elderly Tlingit weavers, rather than in the modern way.

RIGHT: In this photo, taken in 1899, a Tlingit woman works on sealskins to make them soft on the inside. (NMAI N36578)

For all Alaska Natives, it has traditionally been the duty of the mother and wife to make outfits for her family. Beautiful clothing allowed the woman to show off her skill, but in creating warm and durable outfits, she also expressed the love she felt for her family. Well-made clothes brought respect and admiration to their makers—and they could mean the difference between life and death during the cold winter months.

*E*very summer Thomas and I spend lots of time with our dad. Usually we start off at his house in Hoonah.

Hoonah is a village on Chichagof Island (pronounced CHITCH-ah-goff) that has been a Tlingit settlement for more than a century. A lot of my cousins, aunts, and uncles live there. Houses line the main street along the water and spread up the hills. There are a couple of stores and boat harbors. One of my favorite things to do in Hoonah is to look for treasures along the beach when the tide is low. It's easy to find sea glass and pieces of china buried in the mud.

At our dad's house, we choose the clothes we'll need for berry picking and fishing. Then we get in his skiff and head across a body of water called the Icy Strait (it isn't icy most of the year) either to Excursion Inlet or to our cabin near Gustavus.

A photograph of Hoonah taken around 1900. The house in the middle has a clan crest painted on the front. (NMAI P19894)

RIGHT: Hoonah today.

LEFT: Lydia and her dad in the skiff they and Thomas use to travel across the Icy Strait.

BOTTOM RIGHT: Lydia and her friend Cheyenne Hill, looking for treasures at low tide near a pier in Hoonah.

Our cabin near Gustavus is on a rocky beach that is about thirty feet away from a small river that empties into the Icy Strait. There are trails in the woods all around, and you can hike about a mile up to a waterfall. On the trail you have to watch out for moose and bears, because the bushes are thick and these animals don't like to be surprised. I've become pretty good at spotting their tracks. If they hear you coming, they'll stay out of the way most of the time. There also are mudflats in front of our cabin where we dig for clams. Sometimes we have to bring our boat up the river because the mudflats are so shallow that we can't land on the beach.

Lydia inside their cabin with a bear skull her dad found nearby.

ABOVE: Lydia and her father watch for bears and moose on the hiking trail to the waterfall.

LEFT: Lydia walking in a creek beside the cabin her dad built.

RIGHT: Lydia above the waterfall in the mountains near the cabin.

Excursion Inlet from the air.

An inlet is a place where a sliver of the sea extends into a crack in the coastline. Sometimes an inlet can be big, but Excursion Inlet is only a couple of miles long and less than a mile wide. Before Europeans arrived, many Tlingit families used the area as a base camp. Creeks and rivers were filled with salmon making their way upstream to spawn, and berries grew in many different parts of the inlet. Because there was only one waterway in, anyone who tried to enter would be seen by a lookout, so Excursion Inlet was a very safe place.

Tlingits lived in Excursion Inlet throughout the year. During the summer, we caught fish and seal and hunted deer, drying the meat. We also gathered all kinds of berries. During the winter, up to five families lived together in each wooden, rectangular clan house. The women made clothes out of tanned deer and seal hides, while the men mended their broken tools and fishing nets. It was like this for a long time.

A Tlingit seal hunters' camp at Yakutat Bay, about 200 miles north of Excursion Inlet. Sealskins, which were tanned and used to make warm clothing, are stretched across wooden frames to dry. This photo was taken in 1899. Today seal hunting has been greatly reduced, but Tlingits still eat seal oil drizzled over potatoes or dried fish. (NMAI P10973)

In the early 1900s, Excursion Inlet became the site of a fish cannery. The cannery buys salmon from fishing boats, cleans and processes the fish, and puts it into cans. The land at Excursion Inlet is no longer the community property that the Tlingit people once shared. Grandma Katherine and her brothers and sisters grew up in the village of Hoonah, which is about three hours across the water, but they spent their summers at Excursion Inlet. There they would work in the cannery and catch and dry fish on their own. Many of my other relatives have worked in the cannery, too.

My family is lucky. We still own a house at Excursion Inlet. My great-grandpa built it more than eighty years ago. I have been going to Excursion Inlet every summer since I was a baby. It's the same for my brother and many of my cousins.

OPPOSITE LEFT: Lydia's family's house at Excursion Inlet.

ABOVE: The fish cannery at Excursion Inlet.

t Excursion Inlet, we usually stay at the family house. We swim in the big lake and go fishing in the creeks and rivers for different kinds of salmon. My dad has taught Thomas and me how to use traditional gaff hooks. Tlingits used gaff hooks long before the fishing rod and reel were invented. Fishing that way takes a little practice and a lot of patience. Last summer we caught seven sockeye salmon with our gaff hooks! We eat some of the fish we catch right away. The rest of it we put up.

Lydia and Thomas on a swing set used by all the kids at Excursion Inlet.

LEFT: Lydia with her gaff hook, standing on a section of a big concrete pipe.

RIGHT: Lydia's dad teaches her to fish with a gaff hook.

"*P*utting up" means preparing or drying out food so that it lasts during the winter months. This is a very old Tlingit tradition. Berries can be made into jam or jelly or you can put them in the freezer. They don't taste as fresh as when you pick them right off the bush, but they're still good.

We put up fish, mainly salmon, by drying it in the smokehouse. The smokehouse at Excursion Inlet has been used by everyone in our family since it was built in the 1940s. It's a small house with one door. Racks line the walls, and poles hang from the ceiling. A big stove sits in the middle.

We cut our fish into strips. My dad makes a special brine of water, salt, and a little bit of brown sugar. We soak the strips of fish in the brine and hang them from the poles in the smokehouse. Then we build a fire in the stove.

OPPOSITE TOP: The smokehouse at Excursion Inlet.

OPPOSITE BOTTOM: Freshly caught salmon hang from hooks in the smokehouse. The fire has not yet been lighted. (Courtesy of the Mills family)

Usually our family uses hemlock and alder wood for the fire. Other Tlingits might choose a different wood, depending on how they want their fish to taste. We cut up the branches and wrap them into bundles. After the fire is blazing, we stuff the bundles into the fire. The fresh leaves make a lot of smoke. The fire dries the fish, and the smoke adds flavor.

For smoked salmon, you have to make this kind of fire several times a day for three to five days. After the fish is as dry as we want it, we take it down and cut the strips into smaller pieces. Then we put them into cans or jars. A teaspoon of oil helps to keep the fish from drying out. Before we had metal cans or mason jars, Tlingits wrapped the pieces of fish into small cloth bundles and stored them in cool, dry, dark places.

After all the fish is in containers, it's time to seal the lids. We put a big pot on the stove and fill it with water. We put the containers in the water and then let them boil for about three hours. We want to make sure that the fish is cooked through and that the seal on the jar will last through the whole winter. Then we have smoked salmon to eat or give away as gifts. My favorite way to eat it is with white rice and soy sauce. But in general my favorite food is roasted fish tails or deer ribs with sweet-and-sour sauce. Yummy!

OPPOSITE TOP: Salmon being dried in the smokehouse at Excursion Inlet. (Courtesy of the Mills family)

OPPOSITE BOTTOM: Lydia's dad teaches her to seal salmon cans. This photo was taken when Lydia was a little younger. (Courtesy of the Mills family)

ABOVE: Lydia on the dock at Neva Lake, at Excursion Inlet.

OPPOSITE RIGHT: Lydia in the doorway of the smokehouse at Excursion Inlet.

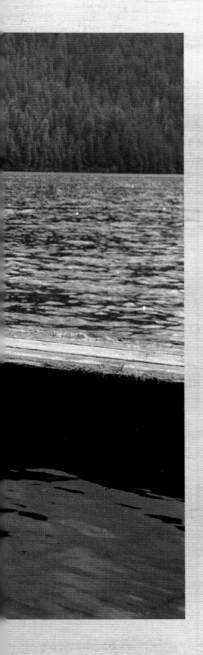

There are other things to collect at Excursion Inlet. My dad showed Thomas and me how to collect cockles, mussels, clams, and chitons from the beach rocks when the tide is low. We call chitons gumboots. You have to be very careful when you're using a knife or a flat screwdriver to pry them off the rocks. Gumboots are black and kind of chewy. You can eat them on the beach or take them home and cook them. They're good for you because they have lots of iron. I like to dip them in seal oil to give them some flavor. I also like gumboots because they have little shells that you can string to make necklaces.

Exploring tidepools and the shallow parts of Neva Lake is one of my favorite things to do. In Tlingit history, kids have always helped to collect shellfish on the beach. In my community, we have been doing this at Excursion Inlet for a long time.

A TLINGIT YEAR

*I*n any season of the year, Tlingit people are gathering food and preparing materials for the next season. Although most Tlingits today don't depend on nature for all of our needs, many of us still follow to some extent the calendar of our ancestors.

The calendar varies slightly from village to village, but most Tlingit groups collect the same materials and food in similar ways. One thing to remember is that Tlingits who live near the water and on islands are more dependent on creatures from the sea. Those who live farther inland rely more on creatures from the woods. Even before European traders arrived in the 1800s, a trade system made sure that people living farther inland could get shellfish, seaweed, and salmon from the coast. Those living on islands could just as easily obtain moose hides, rabbit meat, and animal grease from the mainland.

SPRING

*I*n the Hoonah calendar—as described by Lydia's grandmother, Katherine Mills—the Tlingit year begins in the spring, in March. This month is called Héen Taanáx̱ Dís (pronounced HEEN-tah-nuck-DIS-ee), which means "the month when saltwater fish spawn." The men and boys go out deep-sea fishing for halibut, and the women and small children gather shellfish and gumboots along the beaches at low tide. March also is a good time to hunt bears. Since they have been resting in their dens all winter, their fur is very soft.

April is called Kal.átgi Dísi (pronounced kahl-UT-gee-DI-see), or "the month when not much happens" in the Hoonah calendar. Tlingits in other areas would think that there's a lot to do during the month of April. Much of the year's seaweed gathering occurs in April—we lay it out flat to dry on the beach or in the backyard. It's eaten by itself or mixed into a salmon-egg and clam stew. Deep-sea fishing continues in April, as well as gathering shellfish and hunting small game, such as rabbits and otter.

May is a big month for weavers. It's called Kayaaní Dísi (pronounced kuh-yah-NEE-DIS-ee)—"the month when grass starts to sprout." The women dig up spruce root to split into fine strands for weaving baskets, and they collect cedar bark to be shredded and spun with goat hair for chilkat robes and tunics.

Usually, the cedar bark has to be peeled off the trees. May is also the time to dig up roots for medicine. While basket weavers are gathering their supplies, others are still collecting mussels, clams, and gumboots. Deep-sea fishing continues through the end of this month.

SUMMER AND FALL

June is called Atgadaxéet Dísi (pronounced ut-guh-duh-KEET-DIS-ee)—" increasing month, all birds start to lay eggs." It is during this month that the first salmon berries start to ripen, ready to be picked. Salmon berries look like big raspberries that are colored purple, red, yellow, or orange. They're juicy and sweet, and they taste good with milk and sugar. Before we had freezers, berries were mixed with oolichan (candlefish) oil and salmon eggs and stored in airtight boxes. That way, we could eat fresh berries even in winter. June is called the increasing month because nature is about to burst with activity, which creates a lot of work for Tlingits.

July, August, and September are one long month on the Hoonah calendar. It's called Dístlein (pronounced DIS-klane)—"the big month, time to gather everything, time to keep busy." Southeast Alaska doesn't have the twenty-four hours of summer daylight that shines on regions farther north, but the days are very long. For three months, the sun doesn't set until ten or eleven o'clock at night! In July the first salmon start coming back to the streams of their birth, where they will lay their eggs. Berry picking and root gathering are the main activities, but it's the salmon fishing that gets the most attention during this time. Berries are dried, frozen, or preserved with seal oil. Fish is cut up and either dried outside or smoked in a smokehouse. In the old days, smoked salmon was wrapped in tanned leather strips and stored in a dark dry place during the winter. Today the salmon is canned or jarred.

October is called Shaanáx Dís (pronounced shah-nuck-DIS)—"the month to go to the mountains to get mountain goat." By this time most of the salmon have already finished their final journey back home to spawn, and the steady supply of fish has decreased. Men start hunting again, and they prepare to dry elk and seal meat. Women tan animal hides, gather mountain goat wool, and prepare to make clothing, shoes, and toys from the animal skins. By now, the people have gone back to collecting shellfish on the beach in the ever diminishing daylight.

WINTER

November is Kukahaa Dís (pronounced koo-kuh-hah-DIS)—"the month in which you start to shovel snow." Now there is very little sunlight each day, and the weather has turned cold. Any time spent outside is used to hunt, gather shellfish, and catch the last of the salmon. The men also use this time to find large trees to carve into house posts or totem poles.

Most people stay inside. The women sew new clothes, shoes, hats, and mittens while the men repair their hunting and fishing tools, tell stories, and prepare for potlatches.

December is Lkeeyí kei u.eix (pronounced Lh-kee-YEE-kay-oo-ake)—"the month when you can't see the four corners of the house." Most of us don't spend much time outdoors: as in November, we weave, bead, sew, or repair tools and clothing. Hunting and shellfish gathering still occur, but since it is cold and there is very little daylight, we can do this only for a few hours at a time. We begin this abbreviated gathering schedule in November and follow it through January, which is called T'aawák Dísi (pronounced tah-WUCK-DIS-ee)—"the geese month." Since geese stay around all winter, they are the only birds that it is possible to hunt at this time.

February, S'eek Dísi (pronounced seek-DI-see), or "the black bear month," is when the black bears have their cubs. The mother bears throw them out of the den into the snow, perhaps to help them adjust to the cold. The production of clothes, tools, and weapons starts to slow down during February. The focus shifts back to deep-sea fishing, which will mark the beginning of not only the next month but also of another year.

Tlingit people have most of their memorial parties and potlatches during the fall and winter months, just as their ancestors did. The entire summer month has been spent preparing for the winter; food has been preserved both to eat every day and for the food giveaways that occur during potlatches.

Throughout the winter, Tlingits carve wooden art; weave baskets, blankets, and clothes; and tell stories. Today there are fewer and fewer people who still carve and weave. Those that do still collect their bark and roots in the springtime, but now they weave whenever they have time, in any month of the year.